FROGGY GOES TO BED

FROGGY
GOES TO BED

by JONATHAN LONDON
illustrated by FRANK REMKIEWICZ

PUFFIN BOOKS

For Froggy's mother, Maureen
—J. L.

For Jessica
—F. R.

PUFFIN BOOKS
Published by the Penguin Group
Penguin Putnam Books for Young Readers,
345 Hudson Street, New York, New York 10014, U.S.A.
Penguin Books Ltd, 80 Strand, London WC2R ORL, England
Penguin Books Australia Ltd, Ringwood, Victoria, Australia
Penguin Books Canada Ltd, 10 Alcorn Avenue, Toronto, Ontario, Canada M4V 3B2
Penguin Books (N.Z.) Ltd, 182-190 Wairau Road, Auckland 10, New Zealand

Penguin Books Ltd, Registered Offices: Harmondsworth, Middlesex, England

First published in the United States of America by Viking,
a division of Penguin Putnam Books for Young Readers, 2000
Published by Puffin Books, a division of Penguin Putnam Books for Young Readers, 2002

30 29
Text copyright © Jonathan London, 2000
Illustrations copyright © Frank Remkiewicz, 2000
All rights reserved

Library of Congress Cataloging-in-Publication data is available.

Puffin Books ISBN 978-0-14-056657-4

Manufactured in China

It was late.
Froggy was too pooped to pop.
He'd been playing hard at Max's all day long.

"No!" cried Froggy.
"I'm not tired!"

"Why don't you take
a nice bath?" she said.
"We'll make it a bubble bath."

"Okay," said Froggy. "But first I have to find my boat!"— *flop flop flop*.

He looked in the fridge.
"Nope!"

He looked beneath the sink.
"Not here!"

He looked in the
laundry bin.
"I found it!"

And he took a bath—*splash splash splash.*

"Now it's time to put
your pajamas on!" said his mother.
And she wrapped him all
cozy warm in a towel.

"Okay," said Froggy. "But first
I have to find them!"—*flop flop flop*.

He looked on his floor.
"Nope!"
He looked in his toy chest. "Not here!"
He looked behind his desk. "I found them!"
And he put them on—*zwoop*.

"Okay," said Froggy. "But first
I have to find my toothbrush!"—*flop flop flop*.

He looked in the fishbowl.
"Nope!"

He looked in the wastebasket.
"Not here!"

He looked in the cookie jar.
"I found it!"

And he brushed his gums—*brush brush brush*.

FRROOGGYY!

called his mother.
"Wha-a-a-a-t?"
"I bet you want your
huggy," said his mother.

"Yep!" said Froggy.
"I have to find my huggy!"—*flop flop flop.*

"Oh, here it is!
It's under the stove!" *Bonk!*
He gave it a hug and climbed into bed.

"Now it's time to sleep!" said his mother,
and gave him a good-night kiss.
"Okay," said Froggy.
"But first I need a snack! *Then* I'll go to sleep."
And he hopped out of bed—*flop flop flop*.

Munch scrunch munch.
He ate a bowl of flies . . .

then crawled back into bed.

"Now go to sleep, Froggy!" said his mother.
She was getting a little tired herself.
"Okay," said Froggy. "But I'm *thirsty*!
And you have to close the closet!
And open my door just a crack!
And turn the night-light down just how I like it!
Then I'll go to sleep!"

"Oh fiddlesticks!" said his mother,
and got him a glass of water.

"Oops!" cried Froggy,
looking more red in the face than green.
"It spilled!"

"Oh, Froggy," said his mother.
She wiped it up . . .

then got him
another glass of water—
glug glug glug.

Closed the closet—*slam!*

Opened his door
just a crack—*cre-e-eak.*

And turned down
the light just right.
"*Now go to sleep!*" she said.

"Okay," said Froggy. "But first . . .
will you read me a story?"
"Of course, dear." She yawned.

And she read . . .

and she read . . .

and she read. . . till the book dropped—
thump!—
and she fell asleep,
snoring like a horse.

"Good night, Mom," said Froggy.

Then he closed his eyes and went to sleep—zzzzzzzzzz.

ZZZZZZ

"Good night, Froggy!" said Mr. Owl, sitting on a branch.

WHO WHO WHOOOOO